Numerical Index

Song number — Title (recording and number) — Tempo/Energy

1	Leaning on the Everlasting Arms (Red 2)	medium
2	Amazing Grace (Red 4)	slow
3	I Will Sing of the Mercies (Red 8)	fast
4	Trust and Obey (When We Walk With the Lord) (Red 9)	slow
5	He Is Lord (Red 10)	medium
6	Wade in the Water (Red 11)	medium
7	Peace Like a River (Red 14)	slow
8	Praise Him, Praise Him (Red 16)	fast
9	Alive, Alive (Red 17)	medium
10	Wonderful Words of Life (Red 20)	medium
11	Blessed Assurance (Blue 3)	medium
12	His Eye is on the Sparrow (Blue 4)	slow
13	Rejoice in the Lord Always (Blue 5)	fast
14	Down in My Heart (Blue 10)	fast
15	Oh, For a Thousand Tongues (Blue 11)	medium
16	Cast Your Burden (Blue 12)	medium
17	Give Me Jesus (Blue 14)	slow
18	Holy, Holy, Holy (Blue 15)	fast
19	Come, Christians, Join to Sing (Blue 18)	medium
20	From the Rising of the Sun (Blue 19)	slow
21	Lord, I Want to Be a Christian (Green 2)	medium
22	Oh, How I Love Jesus (Green 5)	fast
23	Joyful, Joyful, We Adore Thee (Green 8)	medium
24	The Law of the Lord (Green 9)	slow
25	All Things Bright and Beautiful (Green 12)	medium
26	Praise God From Whom All Blessings Flow (Green 15)	medium
27	Praise the Savior (Green 16)	fast
28	I Surrender All (Green 18)	medium
29	Turn Your Eyes Upon Jesus (Green 19)	slow
30	To God Be the Glory (Green 20)	fast
31	O Come, Let Us Adore Him (Orange 1)	fast
32	God Is So Good (Orange 2)	medium
33	What a Mighty God We Serve (Orange 3)	medium
34	Be Still and Know (Orange 4)	slow
35	Heavenly Father I Appreciate You (Orange 5)	fast
36	Nothing But the Blood (Orange 8)	medium
37	'Tis So Sweet to Trust in Jesus (Orange 9)	slow
38	I Have Decided to Follow Jesus (Orange 13)	medium
39	Tell Me the Story of Jesus (Orange 15)	medium
40	Were You There? (Orange 19)	slow
41	Standing on the Promises (Gold 1)	fast
42	Beautiful Savior (Gold 2)	medium
43	Take My Life, and Let It Be (Gold 3)	fast
44	Softly and Tenderly Jesus Is Calling (Gold 4)	slow
45	My Jesus, I Love Thee (Gold 5)	slow
46	Hosanna, Loud Hosanna (Gold 6)	fast
47	I Know That My Redeemer Lives (Gold 7)	medium
48	For the Beauty of the Earth (Gold 8)	fast
49	I Need Thee Every Hour (Gold 9)	slow
50	I Love to Tell the Story (Gold 10)	fast
51	Stand Up, Stand Up for Jesus (Gold 11)	fast
52	Alleluia Sing to Jesus (Gold 12)	medium
53	My Faith Looks Up to Thee (Gold 13)	medium
54	Just As I Am (Gold 14)	slow
55	O Worship the King (Gold 15)	fast
56	O God, Our Help in Ages Past (Gold 16)	fast
57	The Church's One Foundation (Gold 17)	medium
58	This is My Father's World (Gold 18)	fast
59	When I Survey the Wondrous Cross (Gold 19)	slow
60	What a Friend We Have in Jesus (Gold 20)	fast
61	Angels from the Realms of Glory (White 1)	medium
62	We Three Kings (White 2)	medium
63	Joy To the World (White 3)	fast
64	Silent Night (White 4)	slow
65	It Came Upon the Midnight Clear (White 5)	fast
66	Deck the Hall (White 6)	medium
67	The First Noel (White 7)	medium
68	God Rest You Merry, Gentlemen (White 8)	medium
69	Away in a Manger (White 9)	slow
70	Angels We Have Heard on High (White 10)	fast
71	O Come, All Ye Faithful (White 11)	fast
72	Come, O Come, Emmanuel (White 12)	medium
73	Good Christian Kids, Rejoice (White 13)	fast
74	O Little Town of Bethlehem (White 14)	slow
75	Hark the Herald Angels Sing (White 15)	fast
76	He is Born (White 16)	medium
77	How Great Our Joy (White 17)	medium
78	Infant Holy, Infant Lowly (White 18)	fast
79	What Child Is This? (White 19)	slow
80	We Wish You a Merry Christmas (White 20)	fast

Alphabetical Index

God's Kids WORSHIP™ Songbook

80 all-time worship favorites
arranged for kids and the adults who lead them
by Bob Singleton

COMPANION MATERIALS:

TITLE	ISBN	UPC
God's Kids Worship — Blue CD	1400300487	023755041401
God's Kids Worship — Blue Cassette	1400300444	023755041364
God's Kids Worship — Green CD	1400300495	023755041418
God's Kids Worship — Green Cassette	1400300452	023755041371
God's Kids Worship — Orange CD	1400300517	023755041432
God's Kids Worship — Orange Cassette	1400300479	023755041395
God's Kids Worship — Red CD	1400300509	023755041425
God's Kids Worship — Red Cassette	1400300460	023755041388
God's Kids Worship Gold — Hymns CD	140030332X	023755044723
God's Kids Worship Gold — Hymns Cassette	1400303338	023755044730
God's Kids Worship White — Christmas CD	1400303346	023755044747
God's Kids Worship White — Christmas Cassette	1400303354	023755044754

music typeset by Wayne Yankie, Nashville, TN
prepress preparation by Ric Simenson, Computer Music Services
created, arranged and edited by Bob Singleton
editorial assistance by Paula Singleton

Many thanks to the great people at Tommy Nelson who made this book possible:
Dan Lynch, Christa Horton, Patti Evans, Rodney Hatfield, Patrice Tillman and Suzanne Thompson

God's Kids Worship™ created by Bob Singleton for Singleton Productions, Inc.

www.tommynelson.com
A Division of Thomas Nelson, Inc.
www.ThomasNelson.com

© 2003 Singleton Productions, Inc.
All Rights Reserved.

Foreword

God's Kids Worship™ is a collection of music for kids and the adults that work with them. It's designed to ground kids in the essentials of the faith with fun and performable songs that are easy for parents and teachers. These songs are great for church, choir, clubs, listening on the road, or just anytime!

If you're a Christian Education worker or a children's choir leader, you'll find the collection to be a rich, easy and effective resource for song times and performances. The music in the book follows the split-track recordings, and includes all the words used in the recordings. The songs are in easy keys for kids voices, moving quickly from introductions into singing, with few instrumental solos and breaks. You'll like the ease and familiarity of the songs, while the kids will love the fun, energetic arrangements.

Each cassette and CD is arranged to "drop in and play" with pre-arranged song order groups. Each recording contains 20 songs, which are organized into four 5-song groups. Each 5-song group (1-5, 6-10, 11-15 and 16-20) is organized to flow easily for group singing times. The first 3 songs are fast to medium, while the 4th is always slow. The 5th song brings the energy back up to medium or fast. Feel free to mix and match to easily create your own song groupings!

This organization makes it simple to run song time in Children's Church, Sunday school or clubs. Just put in the CD or cassette and play straight through the preplanned song groupings. If you want to go from song time straight to teaching, do songs 1-4 and end after a slower energy song. If you want to go to skits or more fun after singing, do songs 1-5, or even 1-6 for a longer song time. Do you have less time for songs? Then simply do songs 1-3 or 2-4!

In the book, each song title page includes information to make song selection easy. Under each title on the left, is a tempo/energy indication (fast, medium or slow) of how the song is performed on the recordings. On the right, you'll find the recording project title and song number for easy access on the cassette or CD. The three indexes will also speed finding the right song and recording, too.

While copyright restrictions wouldn't allow us to include every song from the Red, Blue, Green and Orange collections, all of the Gold and White collections are included in this book. I hope you'll find this is a collection of endlessly useful and timeless songs, that you and your kids will enjoy for years to come.

Bob Singleton
creator arranger & editor

Energy/Tempo Index

1. Leaning on the Everlasting Arms

GKW/Red #2

Medium

1. What a fel-low-ship, what a joy di-vine, Lean-ing on the ev - er -

last - ing arms; What a bless-ed-ness, what a peace is mine,

Lean - ing on the ev - er - last - ing arms.

Lean - ing, lean - ing, safe and se-cure from

all a - larms; Lean - ing, lean - ing,

Lean - ing on the ev-er - last - ing arms.

2. What have I to dread, what have I to fear, Lean-ing on the ev - er -

2. Amazing Grace

Slow

(D.S.) 1. A - ma - zing— grace! How
(2.) we've been— there How ten

sweet the sound, That saved a— wretch like me!_____
thou - sand years, Bright shin - ing— as the sun,_____

— I once— was lost but now— am found, Was
— We've no— less days to sing— God's— praise, Than

3rd time to CODA

blind but— now I see.
when we'd— first be -

2. When gun.

D. S. al Coda

A -

CODA

see.

rit.

3. I Will Sing of the Mercies

Fast

GKW Red #8

4. Trust and Obey

Slow

GKW Red #9

1. When we walk with the Lord, in the
(2.) fel-low-ship sweet, we will

light of His word, What a glo-ry He sheds on our way!
sit at His feet, Or we'll walk by His side in the way.

While we do His good will, He a-bides with us still, and with
What He says we will do, where He sends we will go, Nev-er

all who will trust and o - bey.
fear on-ly trust and o - bey.

Trust and o -

bey, for there's no oth-er way, to be hap-py in Je-sus, but to

Last time to CODA

trust and o - bey.

2. Then in bey.

D. S. al Coda

CODA

bey.

5. He Is Lord

Medium

GKW Red #10

He is Lord, He is

Lord! He is ris - en from the dead and He is

Lord! Ev - 'ry knee shall bow, ev - 'ry

tongue con - fess that Je - sus Christ is

Lord, that Je - sus Christ is

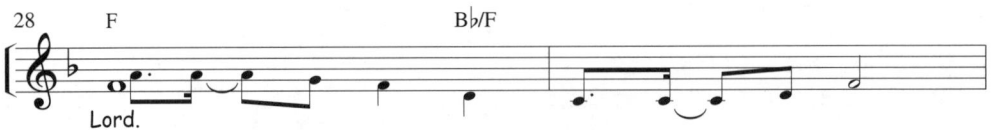
Lord.

6. Wade in the Water

Medium

GKW Red #11

7. Peace Like a River

GKW Red #14

8. Praise Him! Praise Him!

Fast

1. Praise Him! Praise Him!
2. Praise Him! Praise Him!

Je - sus our bless - ed Re - deem - er!
Je - sus our bless - ed Re - deem - er!

Sing, O earth, His
Heav - en's great halls

won - der - ful love pro - claim! Hail Him!
loud with ho - san - nas ring! Je - sus

Hail Him! High - est arch - an - gels in
Sav - ior reign - ing for - ev - er and

glo - ry; Strength and hon - or,
ev - er. Crown Him! Crown Him!

give to His ho - ly name!
Proph - et and Priest and King!

25 C   F   C
Like   a   shep - herd
Christ   is   com - ing!

27
F   C   F   C
Je - sus will guard His chil - dren,   In   His
Ov - er the world vic - to - rious,   Pow'r and

30 Dm   F   G7   C
arms   He   car - ries them all   day   long.
glo - ry   un - to the Lord be - long.

33 F   Bb
Praise Him!   Praise Him!   Tell of His ex - cel - lent
Praise Him!   Praise Him!   Tell of His ex - cel - lent

36 F   F7   Bb   Bbm
great - ness;   Praise Him!   Praise Him!
great - ness;   Praise Him!   Praise Him!

39 F   C   1. F
Ev - er in joy - ful   song!
Ev - er in joy - ful

42

45 2. F
song.   Shout: Praise Him!   Praise Him!

48
Praise Him!   Praise Him!

9. Alive, Alive

Medium

GKW Red #17

live, a - live, a - live for - ev - er more. My

Je - sus is a - live, a - live for - ev - er more. A -

live, a - live, a - live for - ev - er more. My

1.
Je - sus is a - live.

2, 3.
A - live. Sing hal - le -

lu - jah!___ Sing hal - le - lu - jah!___ My

Je - sus is a - live for - ev - er more. Sing hal - le -

2nd time to CODA

lu - jah!___ Sing hal - le - lu - jah!___ My

Je - sus is a - live.

10. Wonderful Words of Life

Medium

GKW Red #20

11. Blessed Assurance

Medium **GKW Blue #3**

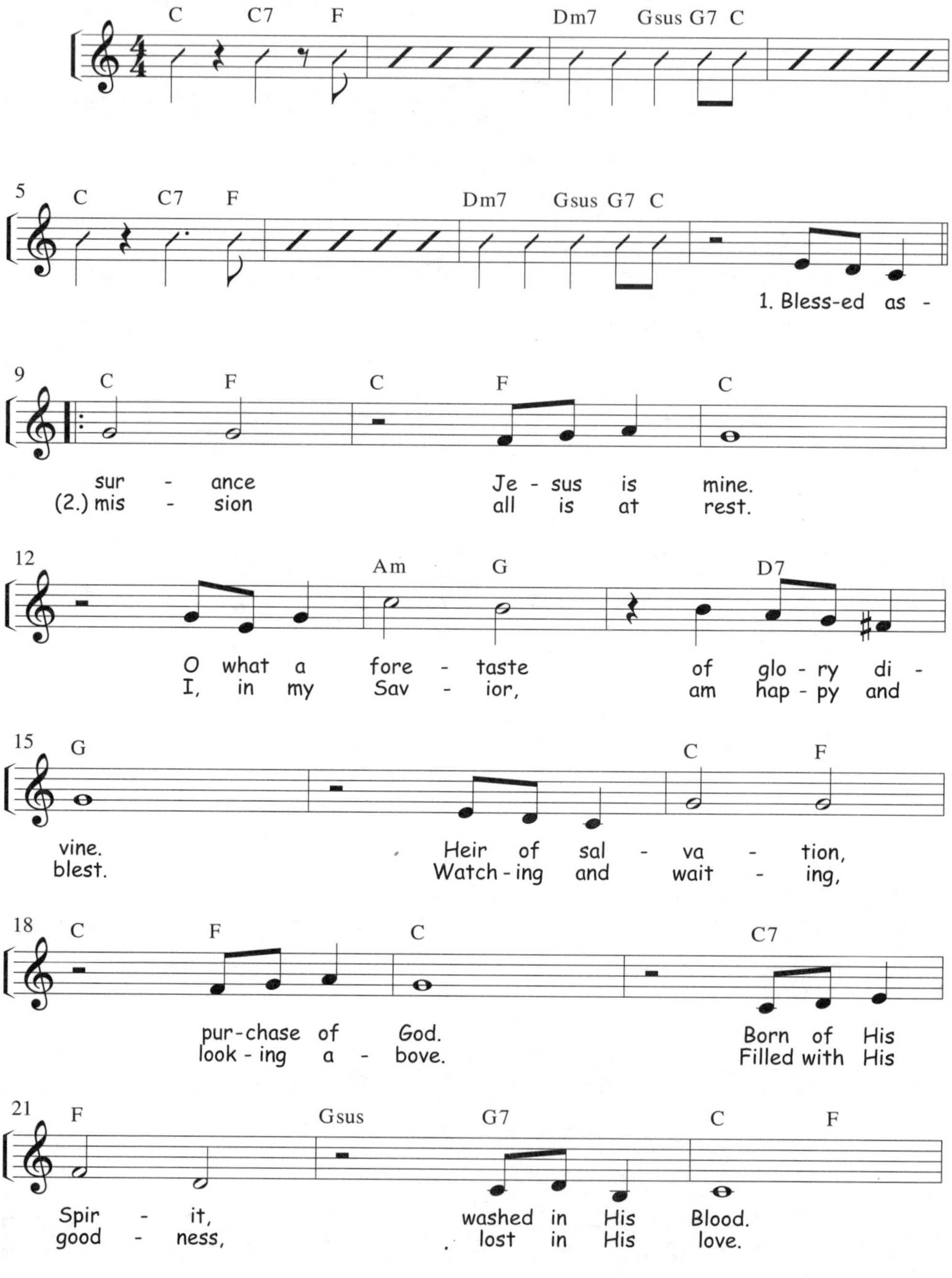

C C7 F Dm7 Gsus G7 C
5 C C7 F Dm7 Gsus G7 C
1. Bless-ed as -
9 C F C F C
sur - ance Je - sus is mine.
(2.) mis - sion all is at rest.
12 Am G D7
O what a fore - taste of glo - ry di -
I, in my Sav - ior, am hap - py and
15 G C F
vine. Heir of sal - va - tion,
blest. Watch - ing and wait - ing,
18 C F C C7
pur-chase of God. Born of His
look - ing a - bove. Filled with His
21 F Gsus G7 C F
Spir - it, washed in His Blood.
good - ness, lost in His love.

12. His Eye Is on the Sparrow

Slow

GKW Blue #4

Why should I feel dis - cour - aged?

Why should the shad - ows come?

Why should my heart be lone - ly, and

long for my heav - en - ly home? When

Je - sus is my por - tion, my

con - stant friend is He. His

eye is on the spar - row and I

13. Rejoice in the Lord Always

Fast

GKW Blue #5

14. Down in My Heart

Fast

GKW Blue #10

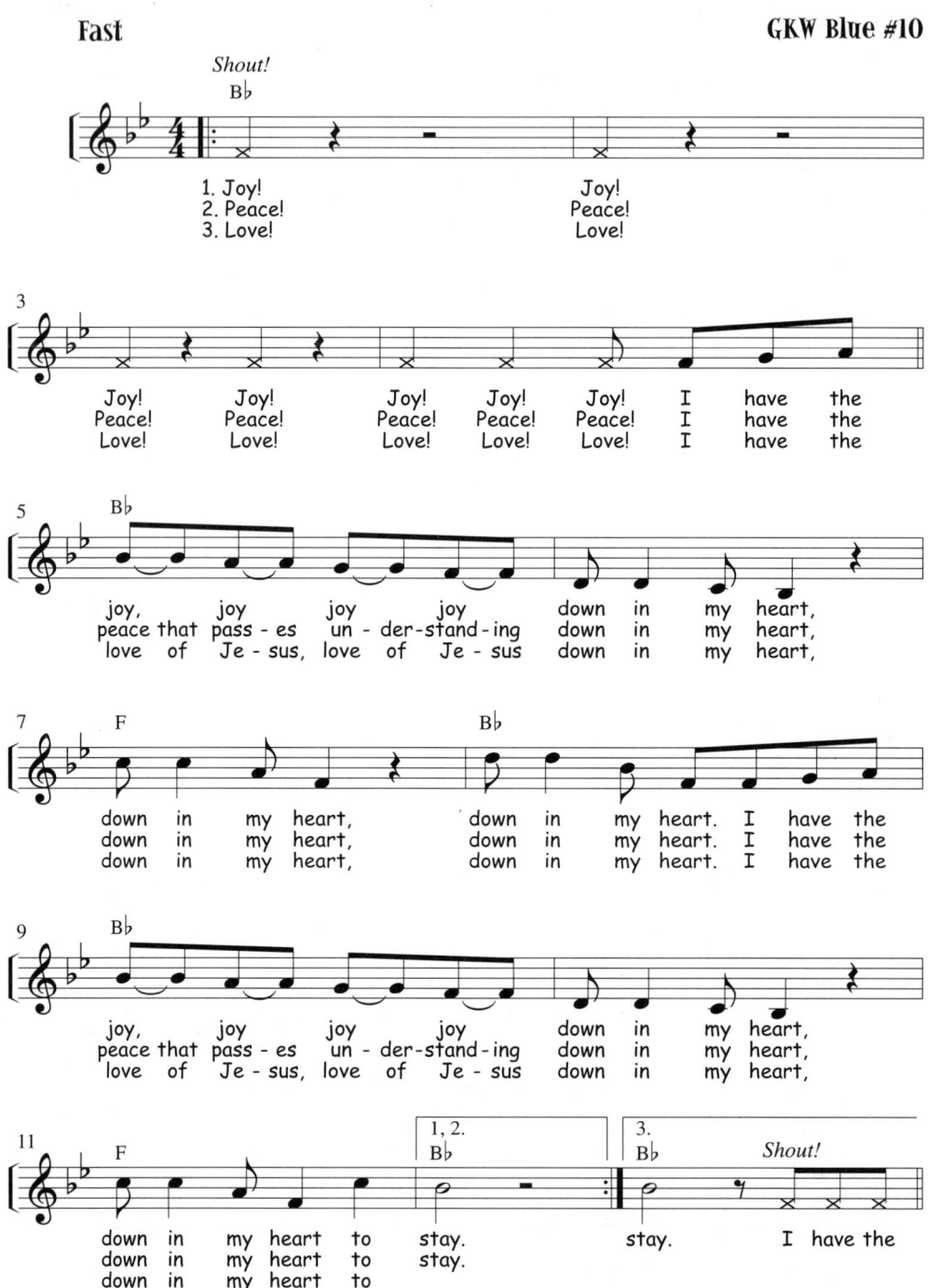

Shout!

1. Joy!   Joy!
2. Peace!   Peace!
3. Love!   Love!

Joy! Joy! Joy! Joy! Joy! I have the
Peace! Peace! Peace! Peace! Peace! I have the
Love! Love! Love! Love! Love! I have the

joy, joy joy joy down in my heart,
peace that pass-es un-der-stand-ing down in my heart,
love of Je-sus, love of Je-sus down in my heart,

down in my heart, down in my heart. I have the
down in my heart, down in my heart. I have the
down in my heart, down in my heart. I have the

joy, joy joy joy down in my heart,
peace that pass-es un-der-stand-ing down in my heart,
love of Je-sus, love of Je-sus down in my heart,

1, 2.   *3.*   *Shout!*

down in my heart to stay.   stay.   I have the
down in my heart to stay.
down in my heart to

arr. & new material Copyright © 2002 Agnes Day Music, BMI
All Rights Reserved. Used by Permssion.

15. Oh, for a Thousand Tongues

Medium

GKW Blue #11

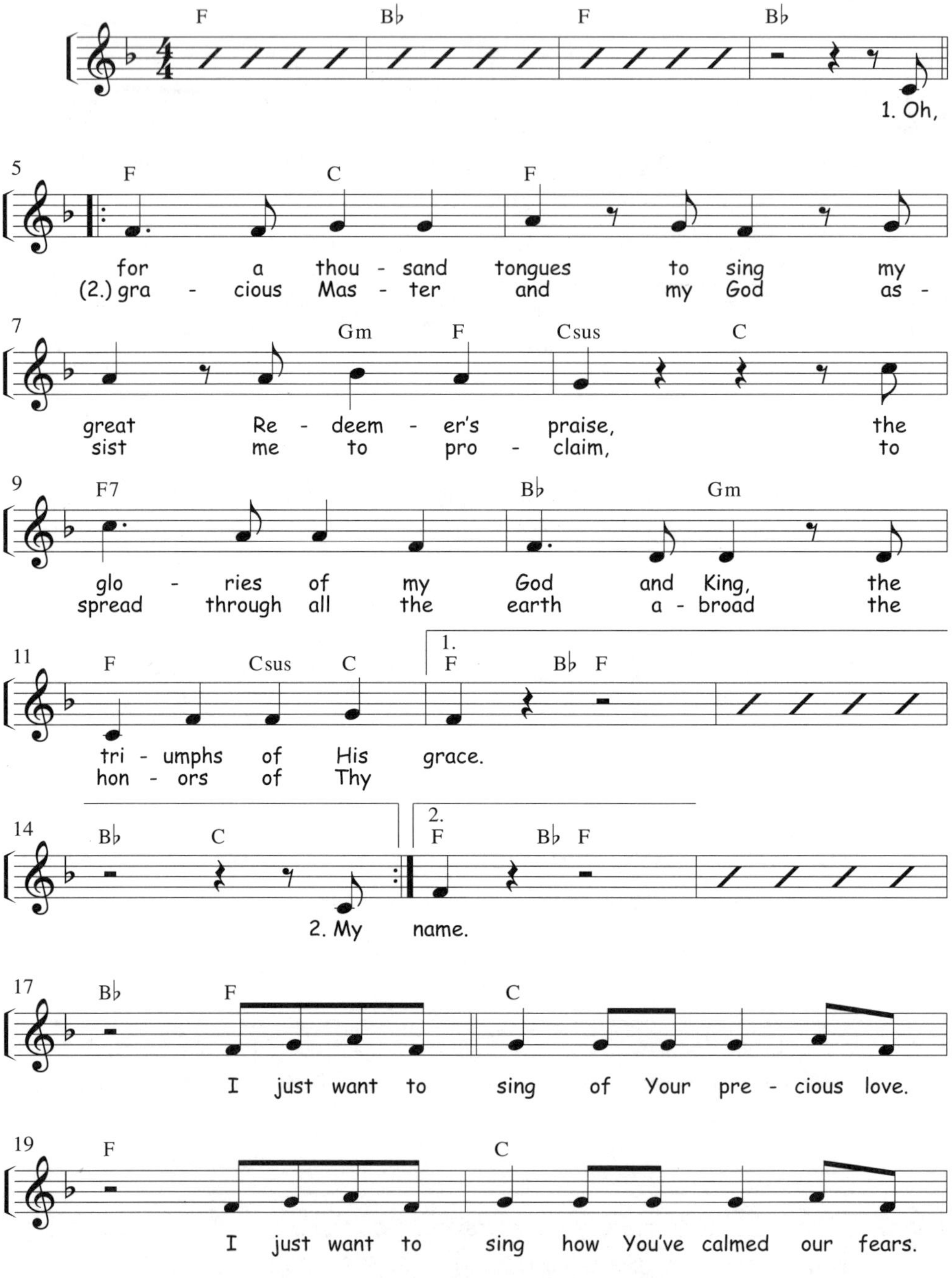

F Bb F Bb
1. Oh,
5
F C F
for a thou - sand tongues to sing my
(2.) gra - cious Mas - ter and my God as -
7
Gm F Csus C
great Re - deem - er's praise, the
sist me to pro - claim, to
9
F7 Bb Gm
glo - ries of my God and King, the
spread through all the earth a - broad the
11
F Csus C
1.
F Bb F
tri - umphs of His grace.
hon - ors of Thy
14
Bb C
2.
F Bb F
2. My name.
17
Bb F C
I just want to sing of Your pre - cious love.
19
F C
I just want to sing how You've calmed our fears.

16. Cast Your Burden

GKW Blue #12

Option: Some repeat meas. 34-41 while others sing 42-end.

17. Give Me Jesus

18. Holy, Holy, Holy

Fast

GKW Blue #15

1. Ho - ly ho - ly
2. Ho - ly ho - ly
3. Ho - ly ho - ly

ho - ly   Lord_____ God Al - might - y.
ho - ly,   though the dark - ness hide Thee,
ho - ly,   Lord_____ God Al - might - y.

Ear - ly in the morn - ing our song shall rise to
though the eye of sin - ful man Thy glo - ry may not
All Thy works shall praise Thy name in earth and sky and

Thee.   Ho - ly ho - ly   ho - ly,   mer - ci - ful and might - y.
see.   On - ly Thou art ho - ly   there is none be - side Thee.
sea.   Ho - ly ho - ly   ho - ly,   mer - ci - ful and might - y!

God in three Per - sons, bless - ed Trin - i -
Per - fect in pow'r, in love and pu - ri -
God in three Per - sons, bless - ed Trin - i -

1, 2.
ty.
ty.

3.
ty.

God in three Per - sons, bless - ed Trin - i -

ty.

19. Come, Christians, Join to Sing

Medium

GKW Blue #18

20. From the Rising of the Sun

Slow

GKW Blue #19

21. Lord, I Want to Be a Christian

Medium

GKW Green #2

22. Oh, How I Love Jesus

Fast

GKW Green #5

Oh, I__ love Je-sus, How I__ love Je-sus.

1. There is a name I love to hear, I
(2.) tells me of a Sav-ior's love, who

love to sing its worth;___ It sounds like mu-sic
died to set me free;___ It tells me of His

in my ear, The sweet-est name on earth.
pre-cious blood, The sin-ner's per-fect plea.

Oh, how I love Je - sus, Oh, how I love

Je - sus, Oh, how I love Je - sus, Be -

cause__ He first loved me! Oh, I__ love Je - sus,

How I__ love Je - sus. 2. It

1.

23. Joyful, Joyful, We Adore Thee

Medium

GKW Green #8

1. 3. Joy - ful, joy - ful, we a - dore Thee, God of glo - ry,
2. All Thy works with joy sur - round Thee, Earth and heav'n re -

Lord of love; Hearts un - fold like flow'rs be - fore Thee,
flect Thy rays, Stars and an - gels sing a - round Thee,

Op - 'ning to the sun a - bove. Melt the clouds of
Cen - ter of un - bro - ken praise. Field and for - est,

sin and__ sad - ness; Drive the__ dark of doubt a - way;
vale and__ mount - tain, Flow - 'ry__ mead - ow, flash - ing sea,

24. The Law of the Lord

GKW Green #9

Slow

1. The law of the
Lord   is   per - fect,   con - vert - ing   the
(2.) Lord   are   right,___   re - joic - ing   the
(3.) Lord   is   clean,___   en - dur - ing   for -

soul.   The tes - ti - mo - ny of the
heart.   ___ The com - mand - ments of the
ev - er.___   The judge - ments of the

Lord   is   sure,   mak - ing wise___ the
Lord   are   pure,   ___ en - light - ning the
Lord   are   true,   and right - eous al - to -

sim - ple.   More to be de - sired are they than
eyes.___
geth - er.___

gold, yea, than much fine gold.   Sweet - er al - so than

Last time to CODA

hon - ey,   and the hon - ey   comb.

1, 2.

3.

D. S. al Coda

2. The stat - utes of the comb.   More to be de -
3. The fear___ of the

CODA

comb.

25. All Things Bright and Beautiful

Medium

GKW Green 12

26. Praise God from Whom All Blessings Flow

Medium

GKW Green #15

Praise God from whom all bless-ings flow,

Praise Him, all crea-tures here be - low, Praise Him a - bove, ye heav'n - ly host, Praise Fa - ther, Son and Ho - ly Ghost. Praise Ghost. Praise God from whom all bless-ings flow,

27. Praise the Savior

GKW Green #16

Fast

28. I Surrender All

GKW Green #18

Medium

29. Turn Your Eyes Upon Jesus

GKW Green #19

Slow

30. To God Be the Glory

Fast

GKW Green #20

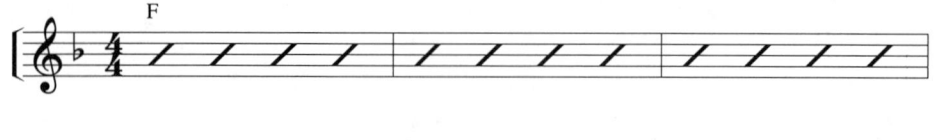

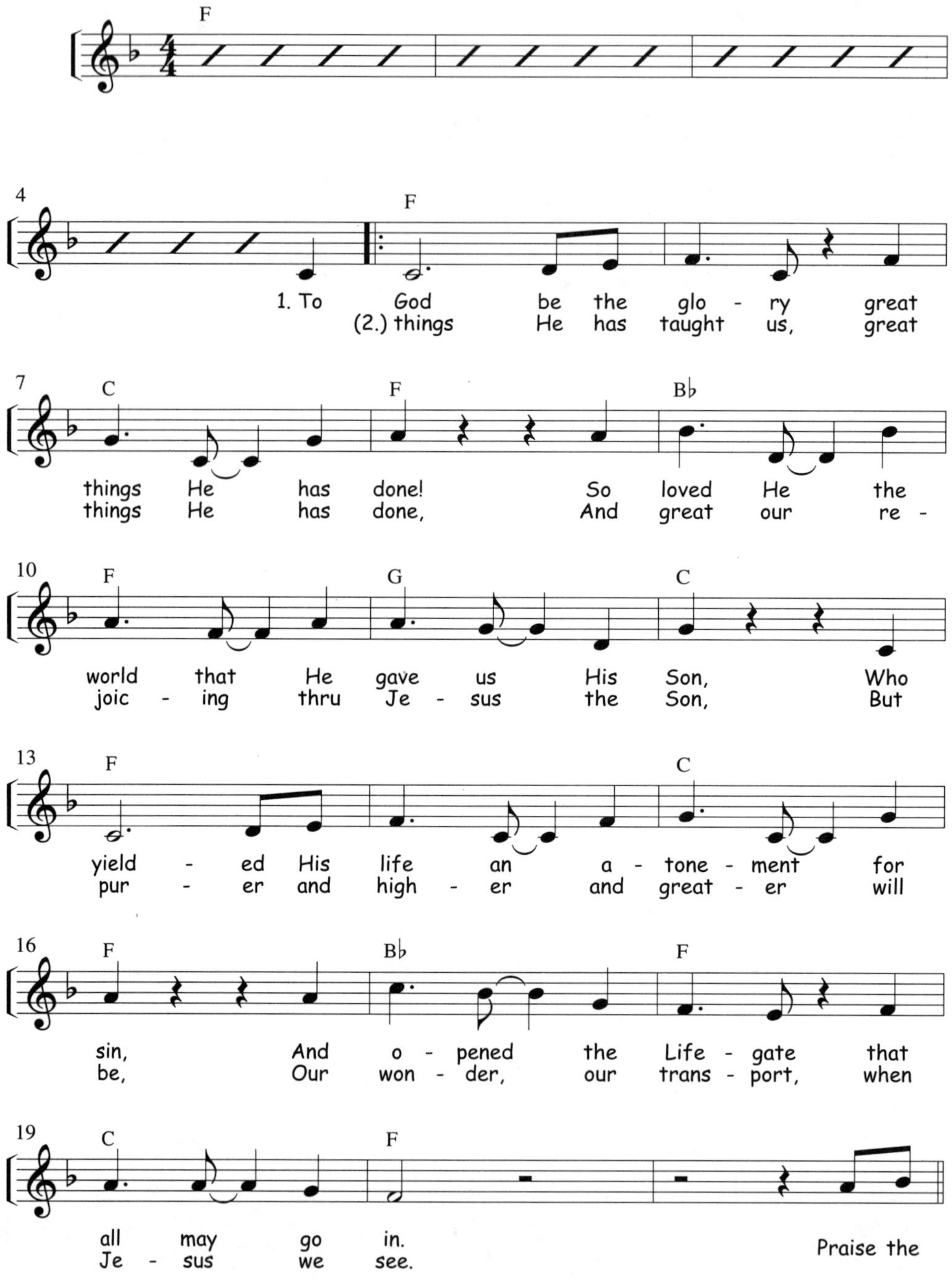
F
4
F
1. To God be the glo - ry great
(2.) things He has taught us, great
7
C F B♭
things He has done! So loved He the
things He has done, And great our re -
10
F G C
world that He gave us His Son, Who
joic - ing thru Je - sus the Son, But
13
F C
yield - ed His life an a - tone - ment for
pur - er and high - er and great - er will
16
F B♭ F
sin, And o - pened the Life - gate that
be, Our won - der, our trans - port, when
19
C F
all may go in.
Je - sus we see.
Praise the

31. O Come, Let Us Adore Him

Fast

GKW Orange #1

32. God Is So Good

Medium

GKW Orange #2

33. What a Mighty God We Serve

Medium

GKW Orange #3

34. Be Still and Know

35. Heavenly Father, I Appreciate You

Fast

GKW Orange #5

36. Nothing but the Blood of Jesus

Medium

GKW Orange #8

37. 'Tis So Sweet to Trust in Jesus

Slow

GKW Orange #9

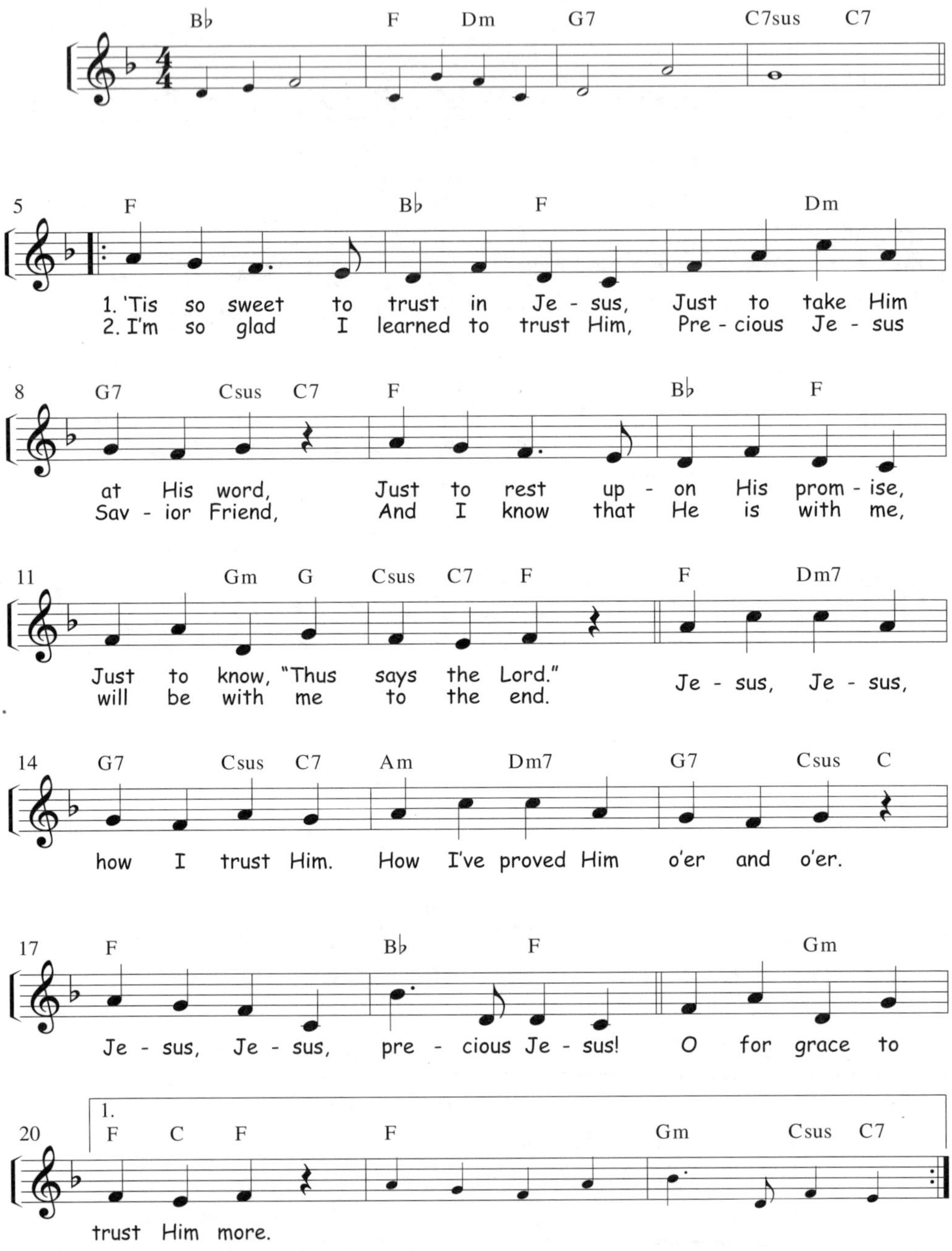

B♭ F Dm G7 C7sus C7
5
F B♭ F Dm
1. 'Tis so sweet to trust in Je - sus, Just to take Him
2. I'm so glad I learned to trust Him, Pre - cious Je - sus
8
G7 Csus C7 F B♭ F
at His word, Just to rest up - on His prom - ise,
Sav - ior Friend, And I know that He is with me,
11
Gm G Csus C7 F F Dm7
Just to know, "Thus says the Lord."
will be with me to the end.
Je - sus, Je - sus,
14
G7 Csus C7 Am Dm7 G7 Csus C
how I trust Him. How I've proved Him o'er and o'er.
17
F B♭ F Gm
Je - sus, Je - sus, pre - cious Je - sus! O for grace to
20
1.
F C F F Gm Csus C7
trust Him more.

trust Him more.   'Tis   so   sweet,   'Tis   so sweet   to

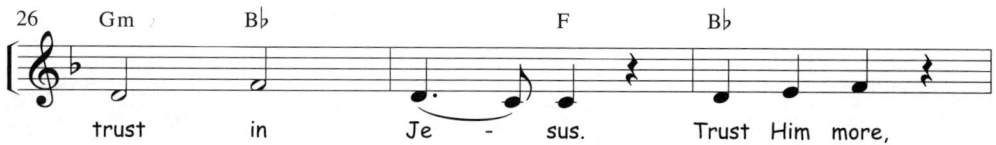

trust   in   Je   -   sus.   Trust Him   more,

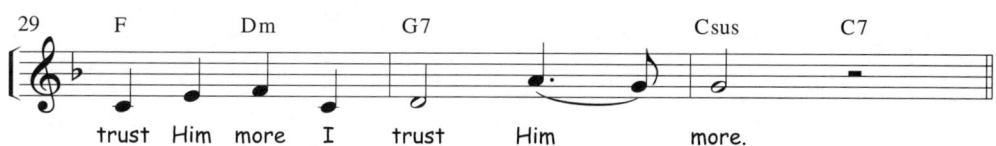

trust Him   more   I   trust   Him   more.

Je - sus,   Je - sus,   how   I   trust Him.   How I've proved Him

o'er   and   o'er.   Je - sus, Je - sus,   pre - cious Je - sus!

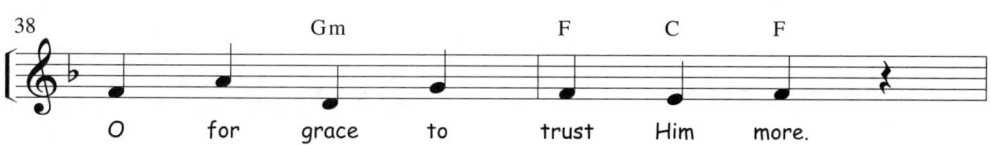

O   for   grace   to   trust   Him   more.

O   for   grace   to   trust   Him   more.

38. I Have Decided to Follow Jesus

GKW Orange #13

Medium

39. Tell Me the Story of Jesus

Medium

(D.S.)
1. Tell me the sto - ry of Je - sus, write on my heart ev - 'ry word, Tell me the sto - ry most pre - cious, sweet - est that ev - er was heard.
2. Fast - ing a - lone in the des - ert, tell of the days that are past, How for our sins He was tempt - ed, yet was tri - um - phant at last.

3rd time to CODA

Tell how the an - gels in cho - rus sang as they wel - comed His birth, "Glo - ry to God in the high - est!
Tell of the years of His la - bor, Tell of the sor - row He bore, He was des - pised and af - flict - ed,

1.
Peace and good ti - dings on earth." poor.
Home - less re - ject - ed and_____

2. D. S. al Coda

CODA

heard. Tell me__ the sto - ry, tell me__ the sto - ry, tell me__ the sto - ry__ of Je - sus.

40. Were You There?

Slow

GKW Orange #19

41. Standing on the Promises of God

Fast

GKW Gold #1

1. Stand-ing on the prom-is-es of
2. Stand-ing on the prom-is-es of

Christ my King, Thro' e-ter-nal a-ges let His
Christ the Lord, Bound to Him e-ter-nal-ly by

prais-es ring; Glo-ry in the high-est, I will
love's strong cord, O-ver-com-ing dai-ly with the

shout and sing, Stand-ing on the prom-is-es of God.
Spir-it's sword, Stand-ing on the prom-is-es of God.

Stand - ing, stand - ing, Stand-ing on the prom-is-es of

God my Sav-ior; Stand - ing, stand - ing, I'm

stand-ing on the prom-is-es of God.

42. Beautiful Savior

Medium

GKW Gold #2

43. Take My Life and Let It Be

Fast

GKW Gold #3

Verse lyrics:

1. Take my life, and let it be Con - se - crat - ed, Lord, to Thee; Take my hands and let them move At the im - pulse of Thy love. At the im - pulse of Thy love.

2. Take my feet, and let them be Swift and beau - ti - ful for Thee; Take my voice and let me sing Al - ways, on - ly, for my King. Al - ways, on - ly, for my King.

44. Softly and Tenderly

Slow

GKW Gold #4

1. Soft - ly and ten - der - ly Je - sus is call - ing, Call - ing for
2. Oh! for the won - der - ful love He has prom - ised, Prom - ised for

you and for me; See, at the door - way He's
you and for me; Tho' we have sinned He has

wait - ing and watch-ing, Watch-ing for you and for me.
mer - cy and par-don, Par - don for you and for me.

Come home, come home, You who are wea-ry come home; Ear - nest-ly,

ten - der-ly, Je - sus is call-ing, Call - ing, O

sin-ner, come home! home!

Call - ing, O sin - ner, come home!

45. My Jesus, I Love Thee

Slow

GKW Gold #5

1. My

Je - sus, I love Thee, I know Thou art
(2.) love Thee be - cause Thou hast first lov - ed

mine; For Thee, all the fol - lies of
me, And pur - chased my par - don on

sin I re - sign; My gra - cious Re -
Cal - va - ry's tree; I love Thee for

deem - er, my Sav - ior art Thou;_____ If
wear - ing the thorns____ on Thy brow;_____ If

ev - er I loved_____ Thee, my Je - sus, 'tis
ev - er I loved_____ Thee, my Je - sus, 'tis

1.
now.
2. I

2.
now.
My____

46. Hosanna, Loud Hosanna

Fast

GKW Gold #6

47. I Know that My Redeemer Lives

Medium

Repeat once

1. I know that my Re - deem - er lives;
2. He lives to bless me with His love.

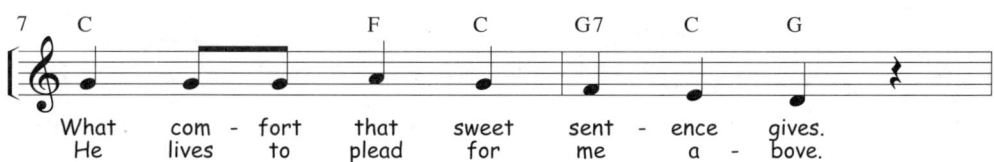

What com - fort that sweet sent - ence gives.
He lives to plead for me a - bove.

He lives, He lives who once was dead;
He lives my hun - gry soul to feed,

He lives my ev - er liv - ing head.
He lives to help in time of need.
My Re -

48. For the Beauty of the Earth

Fast

GKW Gold #8

49. I Need Thee Every Hour

50. I Love to Tell the Story

Fast

GKW Gold #10

51. Stand Up, Stand Up for Jesus

Fast

GKW Gold #11

1. Stand up, stand up for Je - sus You
(2.) up, stand up for Je - sus, Stand

sol - diers of the cross; Lift high His roy - al
in His strength a - lone; Your arm of flesh will

ban - ner, It must not suf - fer loss: From
fail you, You dare not trust your own; Put

vic - t'ry on to vic - t'ry His ar - my He will
on the gos - pel ar - mor, Each piece put on with

lead,_____ Till ev - 'ry foe is van - quished, And
pray - er; Where du - ty calls, or dan - ger, Be

Christ is Lord in - deed.
nev - er want - ing

2. Stand there.

52. Alleluia! Sing to Jesus

Medium

GKW Gold #12

53. My Faith Looks Up to Thee

Medium

GKW Gold #13

1. My faith looks up to Thee, Thou Lamb of Cal - va - ry, Sav - ior di - vine! Now hear me while I pray, Take all my guilt a - way, O let my from this day Be whol - ly Thine!
2. While through life's maze I tread, and griefs a - round me spread, be Thou my guide; Bid dark - ness turn to day, Wipe sor - row's tears a - way, Don't let me ev - er stray far from your side.

My faith looks up to Thee, O Lamb of Cal - va - ry, may Your rich grace im - part strength

54. Just As I Am

GKW Gold #14

55. O Worship the King

Fast

GKW Gold #15

3rd time to CODA

56. O God, Our Help in Ages Past

GKW Gold #16

57. The Church's One Foundation

Medium

GKW Gold #17

58. This Is My Father's World

59. When I Survey the Wondrous Cross

Slow

GKW Gold #19

1. When I sur - vey the won - drous
2. Were the whole realm of na - ture

cross, On which the Prince of
mine, That were a pres - ent

glo - ry died, My rich - est
far too small; Love so a -

gain I count but loss,
maz - ing, so di - vine,

And pour con - tempt on all my
De - mands my soul, my life, my

1.
pride.

2.
all.

De - mands my soul, my life, my

all.

60. What a Friend We Have in Jesus

Fast

GKW Gold #20

1, 3. What a friend we have in Je - sus,
2. Have we tri - als and temp - ta - tions?

All our sins and griefs to bear!
Is there trou - ble an - y - where?

What a priv - i - lege to car - ry
We should nev - er be dis - cour - aged,

Ev - 'ry - thing to God in prayer!
Take it to the Lord in prayer;

Oh, what peace we of - ten for - feit,
Can we find a friend so faith - ful

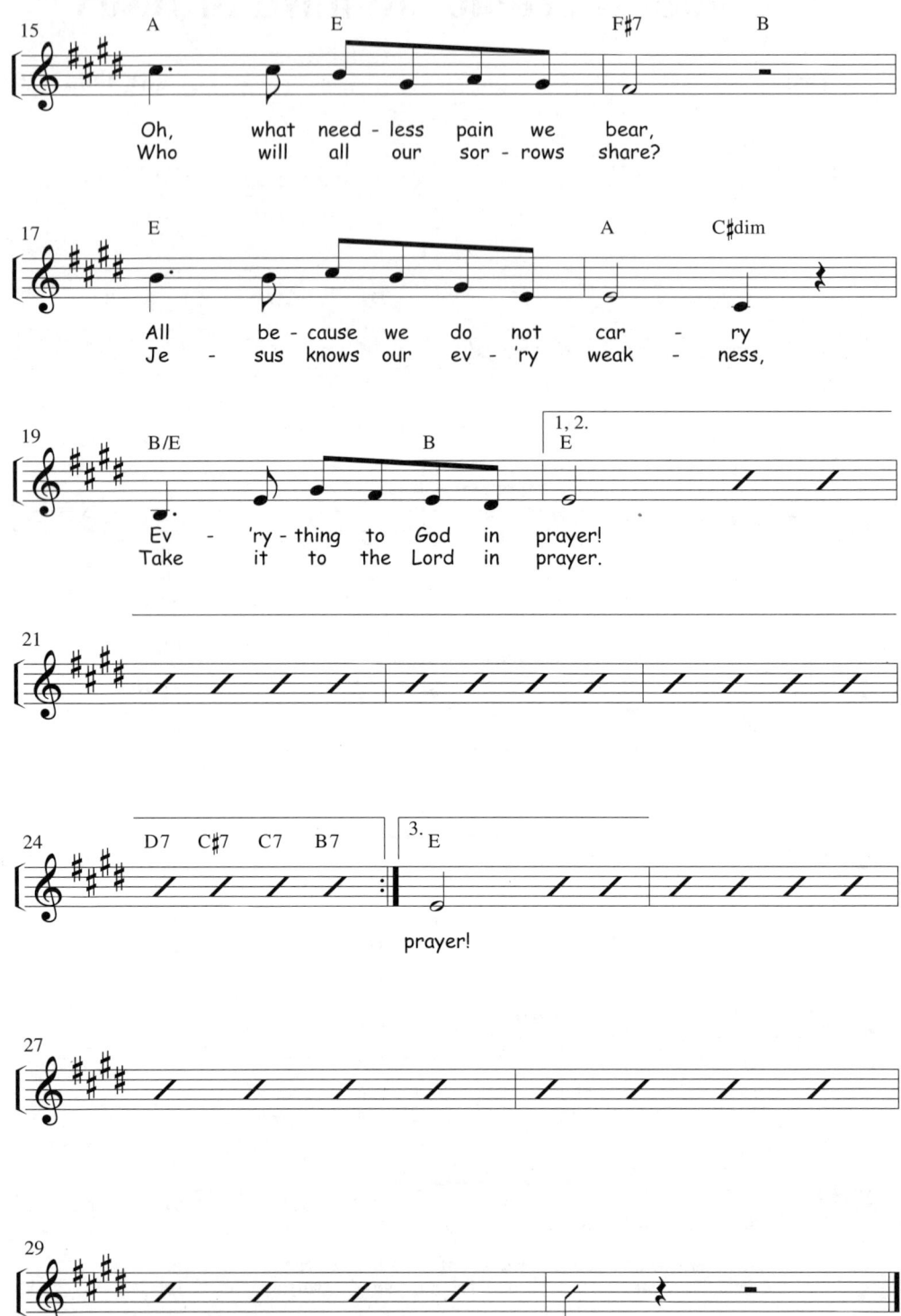

61. Angels from the Realms of Glory

Medium

GKW White #1

1. An - gels from the realms of glo - ry, wing your flight o'er all the earth. You who sang cre - a - tion's sto - ry, now pro - claim Mes - si - ah's birth. Come and wor - ship, come and wor - ship, wor - ship Christ the new - born King.
2. Shep - herds, in the fields a - bid - ing, watch - ing o'er your flocks by night. God with man is now re - sid - ing, yon - der shines the in - fant Light. Come and wor - ship, come and wor - ship, wor - ship Christ the new - born King.
3. Saints be - fore the al - tar bend - ing, watch - ing long in hope and fear. Sud - den - ly the Lord, de - scend - ing, in His tem - ple shall ap - pear. Come and wor - ship, come and wor - ship, wor - ship Christ the

new - born King.

Wor - ship Christ the new - born King.

62. We Three Kings

Medium

GKW White #2

1. We three kings of O - ri - ent are,
2. Born a King on Beth - le - hem's plain,
3. Frank - in - cense to of - fer have I:
4. Myrrh is mine: its bit - ter per - fume,

bear - ing gifts we trav - erse a - far,
Gold we bring to crown Him a - gain,
In - cense owns a De - i - ty nigh,
breathes a life of gath - er - ing gloom,

Field and foun - tain, moor and moun - tain,
King for - ev - er, ceas - ing nev - er,
Prayer and prais - ing, all men rais - ing,
Sor - r'wing, sigh - ing, bleed - ing, dy - ing,

fol - low - ing yon - der star.
o - ver us all to
wor - ship Him, God on high.
sealed in the stone - cold

reign.
tomb.

63. Joy to the World

Fast

GKW White #3

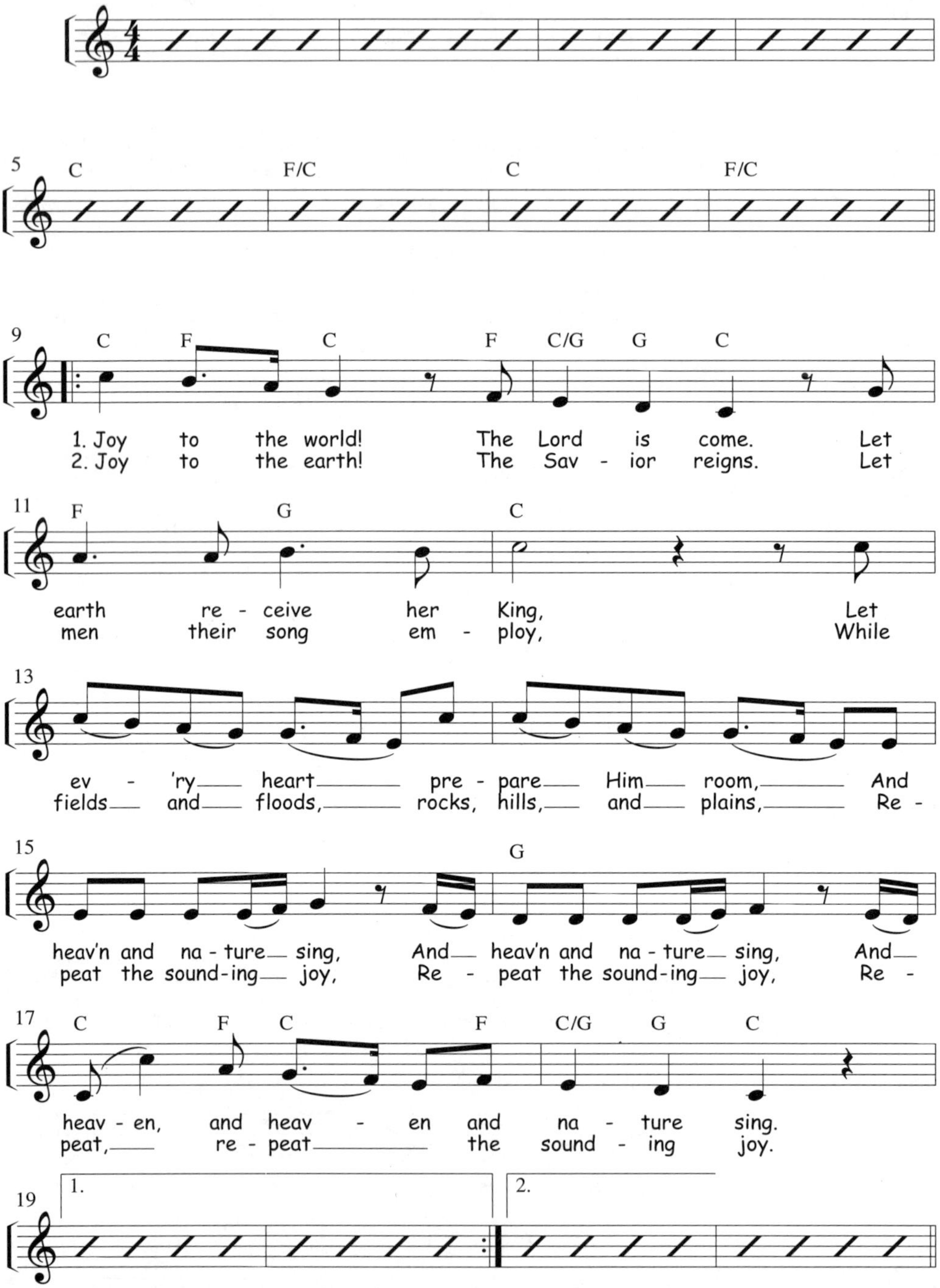

5
C F/C C F/C
9
C F C F C/G G C
1. Joy to the world! The Lord is come. Let
2. Joy to the earth! The Sav - ior reigns. Let
11
F G C
earth re - ceive her King, Let
men their song em - ploy, While
13
ev - 'ry heart pre - pare Him room, And
fields and floods, rocks, hills, and plains, Re -
15
G
heav'n and na - ture sing, And heav'n and na - ture sing, And
peat the sound-ing joy, Re - peat the sound-ing joy, Re -
17
C F C F C/G G C
heav - en, and heav - en and na - ture sing.
peat, re - peat the sound - ing joy.
19
1.
2.

64. Silent Night

65. It Came Upon a Midnight Clear

Fast

GKW White #5

66. Deck the Hall

Medium

GKW White #6

N.C. *rhythm only*

Ay-oh   Ay-oh   Ay-oh   Ay-oh,

1. Deck the hall with boughs of hol - ly, fa la la la la   la la la la,
2. See the blaz-ing Yule be-fore us, fa la la la la   la la la la,

'Tis the sea-son to be jol - ly, fa la la la la   la la la la,
Strike the harp and join the chor-us, fa la la la la   la la la la,

Don we now our gay ap-par - el, fa la la   la la la   la la la,
Fol - low me in mer - ry meas-ure, fa la la   la la la   la la la,

Troll the an-cient yule-tide car-ol, fa la la la la   la la la la.
While I tell of Yule-tide treas-ure, fa la la la la   la la la la.

Repeat once

Ay-oh   Ay-oh   Ay-oh   Ay-oh,

17 N.C. *(Speak in rhythm)*

Get some hol-ly, deck the hall, get your pres-ents, wrap them all,

19

mark one for Ma, pick one for Pa, fa la la la la la la la la!

21 C   Am   F   C/G   G   C

(3.) Deck the hall with boughs of hol - ly, fa la la la la la la la la,

23 C   Am   F   C/G   G   C

'Tis the sea-son to be jol - ly, fa la la la la la la la la,

25 G   C   D7   G   D   G

Don we now our gay ap-par - el, fa la la la la la la la la,

27 C   Am   F   C   F   C   G   Am

Troll the an-cient yule-tide car - ol, fa la la la la la la la la,

29 F   C   F   C   G   C   C

fa la la la la la la la la. Ay - oh

31

Ay - oh   Ay - oh   Ay - oh.

67. The First Noel

Medium

GKW White #7

68. God Rest Ye Merry, Gentlemen

Medium

GKW White #8

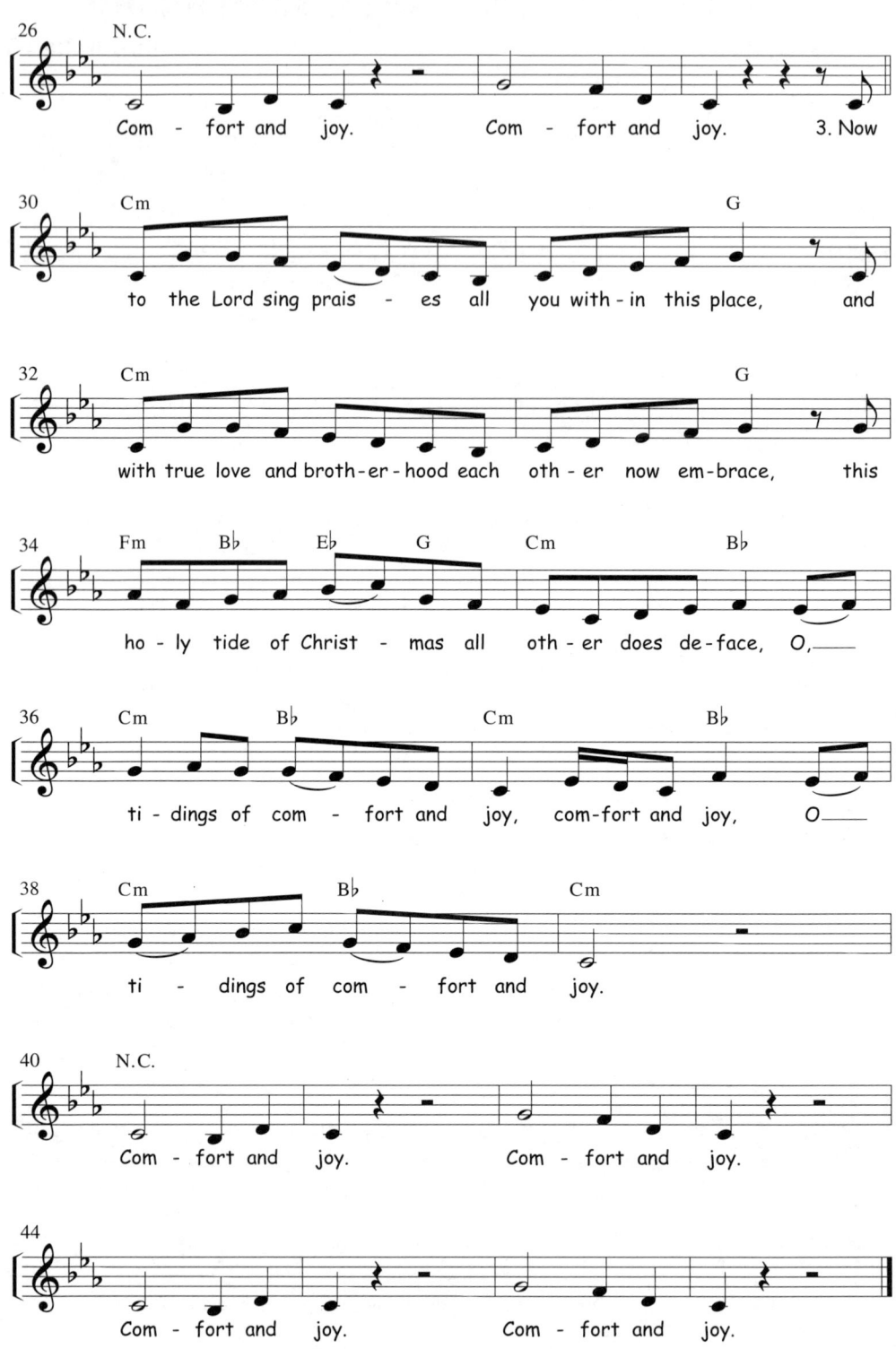

69. Away in a Manger

70. Angels We Have Heard on High

Fast

GKW White #10

1. An - gels we have heard on high,
2. Come to Beth - le - hem and see
3. See with - in a man - ger laid

sweet - ly sing - ing o'er the plains, and the moun - tains
Him whose birth the an - gels sing, Come, a - dore on
Je - sus, Lord of heav'n and earth, Ma - ry, Jo - seph,

in re - ply, ech - o back their joy - ous strains.
bend - ed knee Christ the Lord, the new - born King.
lend your aid, with us sing our Sav - ior's birth.

Glo - ri - a

in ex-cel-sis De - o, Glo -

- ri - a in ex-cel-sis De - o.

o,

in ex-cel-sis De - o.

71. O Come, All Ye Faithful

Fast

GKW White #11

1. O come, all ye faith - ful, joy - ful and tri - um - phant, O
2. Sing, choirs of an - gels, sing in ex - ul - ta - tion, O
3. Yea, Lord, we greet Thee, born this hap - py morn - ing, —

come ye, O come— ye to Beth - le - hem!
sing, all ye ci - ti - zens of heav - en a - bove!
Je - sus to Thee— be all glo - ry giv'n,

Come and be - hold Him, born the King of an - gels!
Glo - ry to God, all glo - ry in the high - est! O
Word of the Fath - er now in flesh ap - pear - ing!

come, let us a - dore Him, O come, let us a - dore Him, O

come, let us a - dore Him,— Christ— the Lord!

Lord! O

come, let us a - dore Him,— Christ— the Lord!

72. O Come, O Come, Emmanuel

Medium

GKW White #12

1. O

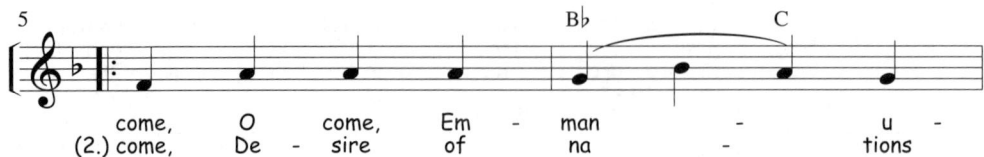

come,   O   come,   Em - man -   u -
(2.) come,   De - sire   of   na -   tions

el,   and   ran - som   cap - tive
bind   all   peo - ples   in   one

Is - ra - el,   That
heart   and   mind,   Bid

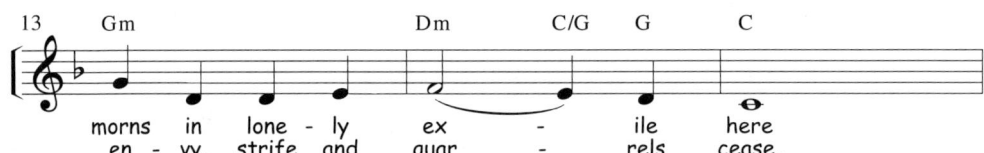

morns   in   lone - ly   ex - ile   here
en - vy,   strife   and   quar - rels   cease,

un - til   the   Son   of
fill   all   the   world   with

God   ap - pear.   Re -
heav - en's   peace.

joice! Re - joice! Em - man - u -

el shall come to thee O Is - ra -

el! 2. O

el! Re - joice! Re -

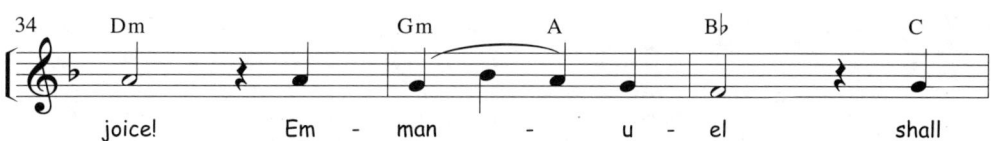

joice! Em - man - u - el shall

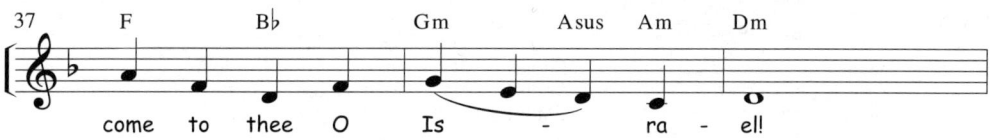

come to thee O Is - ra - el!

73. Good Christian Kids, Rejoice

GKW White #13

Fast

74. O Little Town of Bethlehem

Slow

GKW White #14

lit - tle town of Beth - le - hem, how still we — see thee
(2.) si - lent - ly, how si - lent - ly the won-drous — gift is
(3.) ho - ly Child of Beth - le - hem! De - scend to — us, we

lie! A - bove thy deep and dream - less sleep the
giv'n! So God im - parts to hu - man hearts the
pray, Cast out our sin and en - ter in, be

si - lent — stars go by. Yet in thy dark street
bless - ings — of His heav'n. No ear may hear His
born in — us to - day. We hear the Christ - mas

shin - eth the ev - er - last - ing Light, The
com - ing, but in this world of sin, Where
an - gels, the great glad ti - dings tell, O

hopes and fears of all the years are met in thee to -
meek souls will re - ceive Him still, the dear Christ en - ters
come to us, a - bide with us, Our Lord, Em - man - u -

night. 2. How el.
in. 3. O

75. Hark! the Herald Angels Sing

Fast

GKW White #15

76. He Is Born

Medium

GKW White #16

77. How Great Our Joy!

Medium

GKW White #17

78. Infant Holy, Infant Lowly

GKW White #18

Fast

1. In-fant ho - ly,—— In - fant low - ly,—— for His
(2.) sleep - ing,—— shep-herds keep - ing—— vig - il

bed a—— cat - tle stall, Ox - en low - ing,—— lit - tle
till the—— morn-ing new. Saw the glo - ry,—— heard the

know - ing—— Christ the Babe is—— Lord of all. Swift are
sto - ry,—— tid-ings of a—— gos-pel true. Thus re -

wing - ing—— an-gels sing - ing,—— no - els ring - ing,—— tid-ings
joic - ing,—— free from sor - row, prais-es voic - ing,—— greet the

bring - ing,—— Christ the Babe is—— Lord of all, Christ the
mor - row,—— Christ the Babe was—— born for you, Christ the

1.
Babe is—— Lord of all.
Babe was—— born for

2. Flocks were

79. What Child Is This?

Slow

GKW White #19

80. We Wish You a Merry Christmas

Fast

GKW White #20